MOUSE PRACTICE

story and pictures by EMILY ARNOLD McCULLY

SCHOLASTIC INC.
New York Toronto London Auckland Sydney
Mexico City New Delhi Hong Kong

ISBN 0-590-68267-9

12 11 10 9 8 7 6 5 4 3 2 1   0 1 2 3 4 5/0 · Printed in the U.S.A. 08 · First Scholastic printing, May 2000

Book design by David Saylor · The book was set in 18-point Dundee Bold. The art was created using pen and ink and watercolor on Arches Paper.

Every afternoon, the big kids had a baseball game in the park. So far, they hadn't invited Monk to play.

Then one day . . .

Slugger hurt
his foot.

Hey kid! We need
a right fielder.

Me?

**They figured he'd be fine.
Nobody *ever* hits out there.**

But soon someone did.

CRACK!

UH OH!

Oh, no!

Throw to second!

In the next inning, Monk had to bat.
He was no help at all to the team.

They weren't angry.

It was worse than that. They felt sorry for him.

Dad and Mom tried to help.

They were not what you'd call . . . natural athletes.

So they let Monk try it himself.

It's good to aim _at_ something.

POW!

Monk loved having a target.

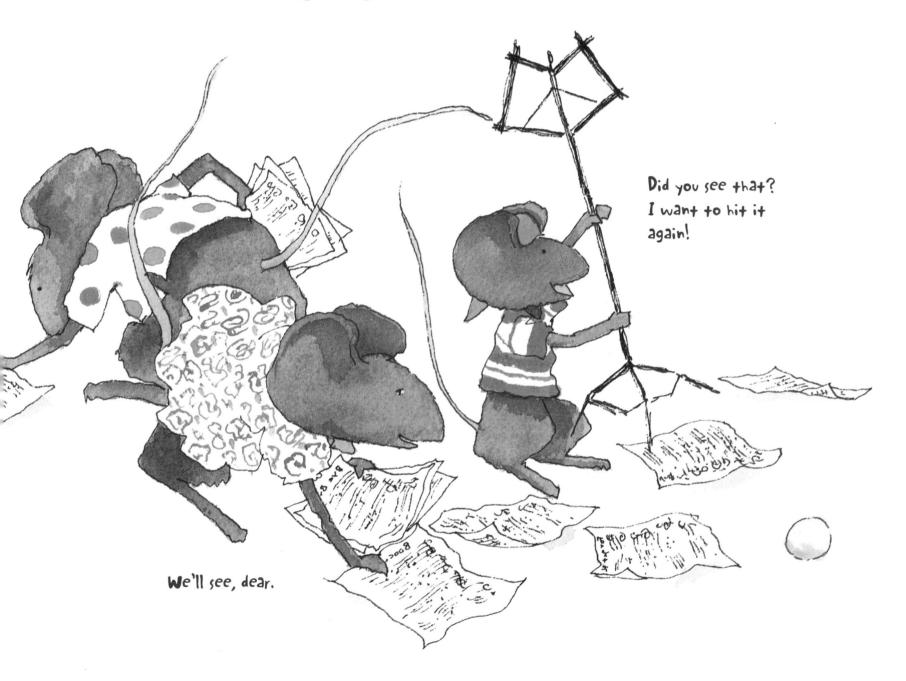

We'll see, dear.

Did you see that? I want to hit it again!

But soon the musicians arrived for their practice.

Monk looked around for something else to hit.
He decided to paint a bull's-eye on the fence.

Monk threw and threw and threw.

After a while, he hit the target.

Monk wanted to work on batting but
no one could pitch. Then he had an idea.

At first, Monk struck himself out.

By suppertime, he could give
the ball some good whacks.

Look at Monk—
he just won't
give up!

Next, he worked on
catching the ball.

A few weeks later, Monk followed the big kids to the park. He took his mitt and baseball.

May I play?

Sorry kid, you don't look any bigger to me.

Hey, Mac, **CATCH!**

SMACK!

You didn't tell us
you could throw
like that!

What an arm!

They sent Monk out to the pitcher's mound.

My dream!

. . . and their team was the only one with a band!